Can you find these animals inside the book?
They have been drawn by children inspired by Miró.

Miró's magic animals

With illustrations including artworks by Joan Miró,
photographs by Lee Miller and
specially commissioned artworks by children

DARCY, AGED 11

NAJWA, AGED 8

JACOB, AGED 5

"I marvel at a little bird that can fly."

Joan Miró

Miró's magic animals

Antony Penrose

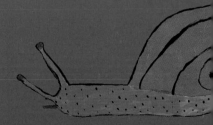

EVE, AGED 10

 Thames & Hudson

My name is **Tony**. This is me wearing my finest horse cardigan. I grew up on Farley Farm in Sussex, England. My father was called **Roland Penrose** and my mother, **Lee Miller**, was a famous photographer.

Both my parents were **SURREALIST** artists.
SURREALISTS make pictures of *dreams*.
A very special friend of my parents also made art
that was *dream-like*, STɼaNGꟾ and MAGICAL.
That friend's name was **Joan Miró**. He came
from Catalonia in Spain, where Joan is Spanish
for John, but we just called him …

Miró's parents lived on a farm, too. Miró painted it. Look at the picture opposite. Can you see the dogs? If you **LOOK** closely you can see mules in their stable, chickens in the chicken run, and even little creatures like a snail and a lizard. The painting reminded me of our farm at home, but in Miró's world it was hot and sunny.

In this picture of the garden, all the vegetables
are in NEAT rows. It looks as if there are lettuces
and tomatoes and lots of other good things to eat.
I was always worried that the donkey might eat all
the vegetables, but he seems *very* well behaved.

The painting opposite has some strange shapes in it, but you can also see a horse with her foal and a farmer with his ox. In Sussex we had a bright blue tractor with orange wheels, but having an ox that you could talk to would have been **much more FUN**. Can you see the rabbit? I don't think the dog has noticed him yet.

EMILY, AGED 7

NAJWA, AGED 8

NAJWA, AGED 8

Miró also painted the farmer's wife. Look how big her feet are! Miró believed that if you want to JUMP as high as the stars you first have to plant your feet <u>FIRMLY</u> on the ground. I felt sure this strong lady could JUMP all the way to the stars. I wondered if she would take the rabbit with her. I don't think the cat wants to JUMP anywhere. Maybe she likes being by the warm stove.

Miró also painted *A DOG BARKING AT THE MOON*.
He put a ladder in his picture. He liked ladders.
Maybe he wanted to give the dog a chance to cLIMB
up to the moon. I wonder if my dad and I were
hoping to reach the moon when we bravely cLIMBED
a ladder at Farley Farm.

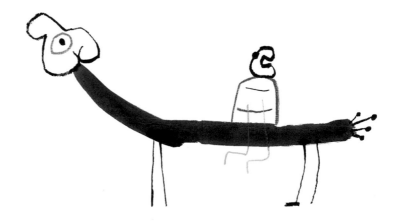

NAJWA, AGED 8

DARCY, AGED 11

Miró moved from Spain to France, so he did not see
his parents' farm very often. Instead he painted things
from his *imagination*. Look at the painting opposite,
called "Harlequin's Carnival". Even though it shows
a **make-believe** world, you can see that it is still
full of LITTLE creatures, just like on the farm.

Miró mostly painted happy pictures. But then **war** broke out. A lot of Miró's paintings showed he was very **UPSET**. He moved back to Spain with his wife Pilar and their little girl Dolores. To escape from all the sadness, he created his own world in his pictures. The painting opposite is called *"The Nightingale's Song at Midnight and the Morning Rain"*. I wonder if the dots are the notes of the bird's song, or maybe they are the raindrops.

NAJWA, AGED 8

Miró came to England and he visited us at Farley Farm. The way he **LOOKED** at things showed he was special. When he saw something that interested him, he *watched* it intensely, like a dog **staring** at a rabbit, except his eyes were always kind. He watched our cows coming in for milking, he watched the birds, and he watched **us**.

Can you see the flowers Miró drew in our visitors book? Is that a bird among them? With his business suits and polished shoes, no one would ever guess that Miró was full of *imagination* and MAGIC. "When I see a tree," he once said, "I get a shock, as though it were something that breathes, that talks."

At the end of Miró's visit we all went to London.
Miró wanted to visit the zoo. Another of my dad's
friends was **Desmond Morris**, a Surrealist artist,
who happened to be the zoo's keeper of mammals.
Desmond asked Miró which animals he would most
like to see. Miró replied, "**LARGE** birds, s n a k e s,
and STraNGe *CREATURES OF THE NIGHT.*"

DARCY, AGED 11

Desmond took us into a special building, where he presented Miró with a new friend. It was a giant hornbill. The bird was **black**, and with its BIG strong beak and tufty crest it looked like something Miró might have painted. He fed the bird some grapes, and it took them *gently*, without nipping his fingers.

NAJWA, AGED 8

Next Desmond brought out a **GIANT** python.
He draped it over Miró, who beamed with delight.
We were all allowed to stroke the snake. It was cold,
smooth and dry. It was nice to touch, but I was glad
it had been given an extra-big lunch.

Desmond had a pet chimpanzee at the zoo called **Congo**. Congo was an <u>ARTIST</u> who painted very exciting pictures. My dad had even made an exhibition of Congo's work. He bought the painting shown opposite and hung it in our home.

We also visited the night animals' house. Miró loved the chameleon, with its swivel eyes that could look in different directions at the same time. Then Desmond gave us a surprise. He held up some food quite a long way from the chameleon. Quick as lightning it shot out its tongue, and with a soft "CLOP" the food was gone. Desmond told us the chameleon had a **BIG** *STICKY* bump on the end of its tongue to help it catch things.

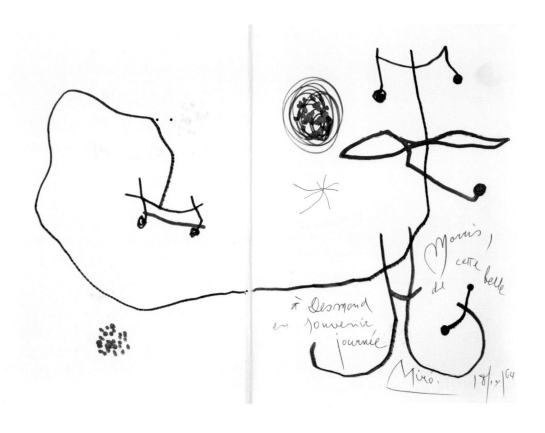

Desmond gave Miró a painting that Congo had made.
In return, Miró made a lovely drawing. It was a picture
of the chameleon! Can you see g**OO**gly eyes and
a long tongue with a **STICKY** bump on the end?

Miró went home to Spain, where he made lots of different types of art. Many of the works he created were UN*U*SUA**L** and MYSTERIOUS. He was happy to be an artist unlike any other, to look with his MAGIC eyes and see things no one else saw.

Can you see any animal shapes
in these sculptures?

Miró and Pilar decided to move to the island of Majorca.
Miró built a lovely studio, and my dad visited him there.

The studio was full of Miró's artworks: his *SQUIGGLES*,
circles and triangles, his stars and moons and LITTLE dots.

Important people now liked Miró's work and his art appeared all over the world. The Spanish people were very proud of him. In his home town of Barcelona, there is even a *fabulous* museum of his work.

By now Miró was old, but
he <u>*never*</u> stopped working.
He even designed the costumes
for a play called "Death to the
MONSTER". The characters
look like creatures that have
escaped from Miró's paintings,
don't they?

Miró died one Christmas Day at the ripe old age of **90**. He is still famous today. But for me he will always be the warm, quiet and friendly man who loved STraNGE animals and made WOnderful worlds for us all to enjoy. I hope you like him, too.

NAJWA, AGED 8

YZABEL, AGED 10

Artroom pp. 1 (left) Jacob Miller; 1 (centre), 12 (above right and below right), 18 (left), 20, 32, 46 Najwa Baig-Derry; 1 (right), 18 (right), 30–31 Darcy Priddle; 3 Eve O'Brien; 12 (left) Emily Rani; 48 Yzabel Jaisa Sampson

Corbis/Hulton Deutsch Collection pp. 28, 29

Getty/Bob Elsdale p. 38

Getty/Desmond Morris Collection/UIG pp. 36, 37 (above)

Robin Lough pp. 42, 44–45 © The Artist's Estate, Courtesy Lee Miller Archives, England, 2015. All rights reserved

Lee Miller pp. 2, 4, 16, 22, 33, 34 © Lee Miller Archives, England, 2015. All rights reserved

Joan Miró © 2016 Successió Miró/ADAGP, Paris and DACS London pp. 6 Double-sided Monolith, 1956. Fundació Joan Miró, Barcelona. Gift of Galerie Lelong; 7 The Farm, 1921–22. National Gallery of Art, Washington, DC. Gift of Mary Hemingway; 8–9 Landscape (Landscape with Rooster), 1927. Fondation Beyeler, Riehen/Basel; 10 The Vegetable Garden with Donkey, 1918. Moderna Museet, Stockholm; 11 Untitled (Donkey), c. 1917. Fundació Joan Miró, Barcelona; 13 (and details) The Tilled Field, 1923–24. The Solomon R. Guggenheim Foundation/Art Resource, NY/ Solomon R. Guggenheim Museum, New York/The Art Archive; 14 Interior (The Farmer's Wife), 1922–23. Musée National d'Art Moderne. Centre Georges Pompidou, Paris. Donation to the French State, 1997. Iberfoto/ SuperStock; 17 (above) Dog Barking at the Moon, 1926. Philadelphia Museum of Art/A. E. Gallatin Collection, Philadelphia; 17 (below) Ubu Roi, c. 1953. Fundació Joan Miró, Barcelona; 18 (above), 19 (details) Harlequin's Carnival, 1924–25. Albright-Knox Art Gallery, Buffalo, NY. Room of Contemporary Art Fund, 1940. SuperStock; 21 The Nightingale's Song at Midnight and the Morning Rain, 1959. Art Institute Chicago. Gift of Mrs. Walter P. Paepcke, 1975; 25 Miró's dedication in Roland Penrose's Farley Farm House guest book, Chiddingly, Sussex, 1964. Supplied courtesy of The Penrose Collection; 26 Birds and Insects, 1938. Albertina Museum, Vienna, The Batliner Collection; 35 Untitled (Snake), undated. Fundació Joan Miró, Barcelona; 39 Untitled (Chameleon drawing), 1964. Private Collection; 40 Project for a Monument, 1979. Photo akg-images; 41 (above) Lunar Bird, 1946–49. Fundació Joan Miró, Barcelona; 41 (below) Solar Bird, 1946–49. Fundació Joan Miró, Barcelona; 43 (left) Poster for Joan Miró's first one-man exhibition at the Galerie Maeght, Paris, 1948. Galerie Maeght, Paris. Fundació Joan Miró, Barcelona; 43 (right) Poster for the exhibition "Le Surréalisme" at the Galerie Maeght, Paris, 1947. Galerie Maeght, Paris. Fundació Joan Miró, Barcelona; 44–45 Costumes for Death to the Monster (Mori el Merma), 1978. La Claca, Spain. Photograph by Robin Lough; 45 (below) Ubu Roi, c. 1953. Fundació Joan Miró, Barcelona; 47 Figure and Dog in Front of the Sun, 1949. Öffentliche Kunstsammlung, Emmanuel Hoffmann Stiftung, Basel Kunstmuseum.

Antony Penrose pp. 23, 24, 27, 37 (below), 39 © Antony Penrose, England, 2016. All rights reserved

For my grandchildren Kahina, Tarik and Amine

With thanks to Ami Bouhassane, Kerry Negahban and Lance Downie at Farley Farm House (www.farleyfarmhouse.co.uk); Sebastian Dewing and all the workshop participants at Artroom Brighton (www.artroombrighton.co.uk); and Jane Wilsher, Alice Harman, Sarah Praill, Jenny Wilson, Kate Duncan, Rachel Heley and the team at Thames & Hudson.

First published in the United States of America by Thames & Hudson Inc., 500 Fifth Avenue, New York, New York 10110

thamesandhudsonusa.com

Library of Congress Catalog Card Number 2015943661

ISBN 978-0-500-65066-0

Printed and bound in China by C & C Offset Printing Co. Ltd

YZABEL, AGED 10

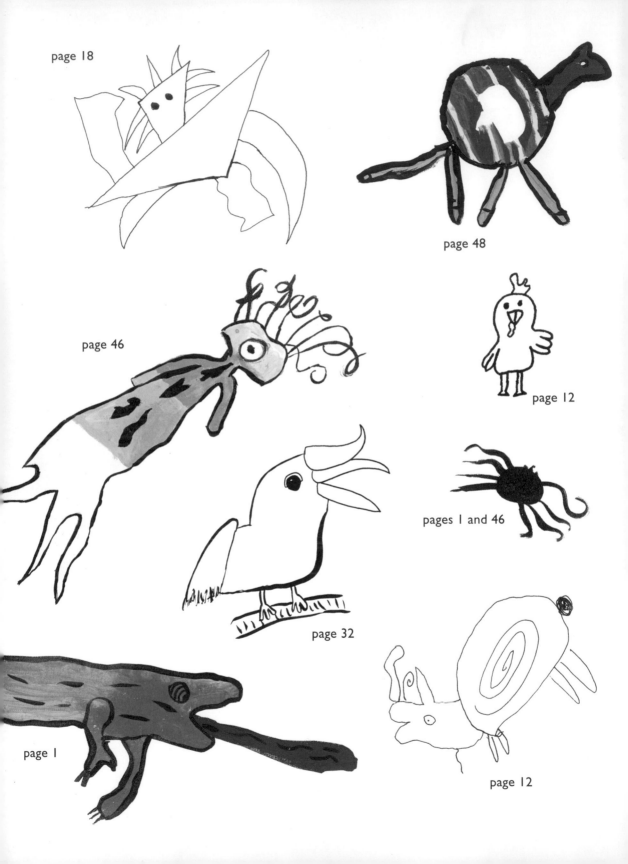

page 18

page 48

page 46

page 12

pages 1 and 46

page 32

page 1

page 12